17
SUGAR CREEK GANG
LOST IN THE BLIZZARD

Paul Hutchens

MOODY PUBLISHERS
CHICAGO

Original Title: *Lost in a Sugar Creek Blizzard*

ISBN-10: 0-8024-7021-1
ISBN-13: 978-0-8024-7021-8
Printed by Bethany Press in Bloomington, MN – August 2010

We hope you enjoy this book from Moody Publishers.
Our goal is to provide high-quality, thought-provoking
books and products that connect truth to your real needs
and challenges. For more information on other books
and products written and produced from a biblical per-
spective, go to www.moodypublishers.com or write to:

Moody Publishers
820 N. LaSalle Boulevard
Chicago, IL 60610

7 9 10 8 6

Printed in the United States of America

PREFACE

Hi—from a member of the Sugar Creek Gang!

It's just that I don't know which one I am. When I was good, I was Little Jim. When I did bad things—well, sometimes I was Bill Collins or even mischievous Poetry.

You see, I am the daughter of Paul Hutchens, and I spent many an hour listening to him read his manuscript as far as he had written it that particular day. I went along to the north woods of Minnesota, to Colorado, and to the various other places he would go to find something different for the Gang to do.

Now the years have passed—more than fifty, actually. My father is in heaven, but the Gang goes on. All thirty-six books are still in print and now are being updated for today's readers with input from my five children, who also span the decades from the '50s to the '70s.

The real Sugar Creek is in Indiana, and my father and his six brothers were the original Gang. But the idea of the books and their ministry were and are the Lord's. It is He who keeps the Gang going.

PAULINE HUTCHENS WILSON

The *Sugar Creek Gang* Series:

1

The first time I saw that big dangerous-looking snake, it almost scared me half to death. It flattened out its ugly head, with its fierce-looking, shovel-shaped nose, and at the same time expanded its neck until it was almost three times as big as it had been. The snake was making a hissing sound like air being let out of a tire of my blue-and-white bicycle.

I stood stock-still and stared at it, my whole body tense with fright. It was lying in a half coil and had been sunning itself on the sandy path that leads from the two big pignut trees above our garden to an old iron pitcher pump at the other side of our farm.

If anybody had seen me staring at that savage-looking, mad-looking, mad-acting, reddish-yellow, thick-bodied snake with irregular-shaped brownish-black blotches scattered all the way down its length from neck to tail, he'd have said my eyes had widened until they were as big as the puffed-out head and neck of that snake.

I was barefoot too, so if the snake had wanted to, it could have bitten my foot or my ankle or one of my ten bare toes—I was that close to it. I didn't even have a stick in my hand as I sometimes have when I walk around our farm, so I couldn't sock the snake the way a boy likes to do when he sees one.

"Hiss-s-s-s!" the big-bodied snake said to me fiercely.

Its ugly head was shaped like a triangle in our arithmetic book in school, and its nose turned up at the tip as if it was trying to smell to see what kind of strange animal I was myself.

As I said, I was scared stiff. My greenish-gray eyes must have been almost bulging out of their sockets as I wondered what on earth to do to kill the snake. If I tried to jump back, would it make a lunge for me and strike me with its fangs?

I couldn't help but think of one of the members of the Sugar Creek Gang whose name is Dragonfly. When he sees something exciting before the rest of us do, he always hisses like a snake, and his own eyes get big and round like a dragonfly's eyes are all the time, which is why we call him by that name.

Well, not having a stick to sock the snake, and not knowing what else to do, and being scared anyway, I let out several screams. In fact, I screamed maybe a half-dozen times, because the snake was not only puffing out its neck and hissing, but its triangle-shaped head was darting in and out in my direction very fiercely.

I must have come to life all of a sudden, for the next thing I knew, I had leaped back about six feet and was looking all around for a rock to hit the snake with. But I couldn't find any because Dad and I had been picking up all the rocks from our farm for years and taking them out of the fields so we could raise better crops.

Even though I didn't find any rock, I did spy a big clod of dirt almost as big as my little sister Charlotte Ann's pretty round head, so I quick stooped, grabbed it up in my big-for-a-boy's hands, lifted it high over my head, and with all my fierce, half-scared, half-mad strength hurled it down toward the snake's shovel-shaped snout.

But as much as I hate to have to admit it, I missed. The dirt clod squished itself into a million particles of dirt and dust right beside where the snake's head had been a second before the clod got there.

And then the queerest thing I ever saw happened. That big forty-inch-long, yellowish-red snake all of a sudden opened its mouth wide and began to twist itself into and out of several kinds of knots as though I had actually hit it and injured it terribly. The next thing I knew, it gave itself a sideways flip-flop and landed on its back, exposing its pretty yellowish-green snake's stomach to the hot sun, which was shining down on both of us.

And the second it got on its back, it all of a sudden quit wriggling and twisting and just lay there as if it was absolutely dead.

What on earth! I thought. *I must have hit it after all!* And yet, I knew I hadn't, because I'd seen my clod of dirt miss by almost six inches. All that had happened to it was that maybe a lot of dust and dirt had spattered it in the eyes and on the side of its angry head and three-inch-wide puffed-out neck.

But there it lay, not making a move and looking like a terribly big fishing worm that was as lifeless as a fishing worm is when a robin has pecked it to death, just before feeding it to one of her babies.

Well, what do you know? I thought. *I scared him to death!* I didn't know if it was my clod of dirt or the way I had yelled at it. But, of course, it couldn't actually be dead.

I looked around and saw a long stick, which I hadn't seen before, and, just to make sure, I picked up the stick and poked at the snake. It didn't even move the end of its tail but lay absolutely quiet.

I don't know what made me do what I did just then, but I all of a sudden felt very brave, sort of like maybe David in the Bible story, when he had killed a giant with one little stone out of his slingshot. I remembered that David was supposed to have had red hair, like mine, so I looked down at that giant shovel-nosed snake and yelled down at it, "Get up, you coward! Get up and fight like a man!"

Having the long stick in my hand, I knew I could kill it, as I had a lot of garter snakes and water snakes around Sugar Creek. So I yelled at it again, calling it a coward to let a ten-year-old boy scare it to death.

And then I got another surprise. From the direction of the iron pitcher pump, which is right close by the stile that we go over to go to school in the fall and winter and spring, I heard a boy's yell. I knew it was the voice of my friend Poetry, the barrel-shaped member of our gang, who was my almost best friend and whose house I was on my way to when I had run into the snake.

"*Who's* a coward?" Poetry yelled to me from the top of the stile, where he was when I looked up and saw him. Then he scrambled his roly-poly self down the stile's four steps and came puffing toward me, walking up the dusty path.

"I just killed a great big snake." I said. "A fierce-looking one about six feet long and as big around as your wrist." It wasn't quite that big, but now that I was a hero, it seemed the snake was bigger than it was. Besides, I wanted Poetry to *think* it was until he got to where he could see it himself. Then I'd tell him I was only fooling, which different members of the gang were always doing to each other anyway.

I stood there, looking at Poetry lumbering toward me. Also I kept glancing at my defeated enemy, wondering how on earth I'd managed to scare it to death.

In a minute Poetry was there, and both of us were standing back about eight or ten feet and looking down at the yellowish-green, up-turned stomach of the snake.

"How'd you do it?" Poetry asked. "What'd you hit him with—that stick?"

"I scared him to death!"

"*Scared* him to death! That's just plain dumb.

You can't do that to a snake. You have to hit him with something."

"I did," I said with a mischievous grin in my mind. "I threw my voice at him, and it hit him, and he just twisted himself up into a couple of knots, like a boy does when he gets the cramps from eating green apples, and he plopped himself over on his back and died, right in front of my eyes. I'm a ventriloquist. I can throw my voice, you know."

Well, it was fun kidding Poetry. Then I told him I'd missed the snake with a clod of dirt but that he'd died anyway.

"Maybe there was a rock in the clod," Poetry said, "and when the clod hit the ground six inches from his head, and burst in pieces, the rock flew out and hit him on the head, and it just sort of accidentally killed him."

That reminded me again of red-haired David. If there was anything in the world I'd rather do than anything else, it was to imagine myself to be somebody else—like a hero in our history books at school or a brave character in the Bible. Right that second, I remembered that David's one small smooth stone had socked Giant Goliath, killing him deader than a doornail. David had rushed up to the fallen giant and had stood on him, and it seemed maybe I ought to do that to my giant-sized, shovel-nosed snake.

"That's Giant Goliath," I said to Poetry, "and I'm David. I'm going to stand on him and cut off his head and—"

"*Stop!*" Poetry said. "He might *not* be dead. Here, give me that stick."

He took my stick, eased himself up closer to the snake, and poked at it. But it didn't move at all, not even its tail.

"It's dead, all right," I said, feeling even prouder of myself than I had been, because of what I had done.

Right that second, Poetry looked at his wristwatch and frowned at it and said, "Hey, we've got to get going! There's a gang meeting down at the spring. Big Jim just phoned our house, and it's very important. He tried to call you, but nobody answered your phone, so I was on my way over to get you."

2

I forgot to tell you that my folks had gone to town, and they had told me I could go over to Poetry's house that afternoon just as soon as I had finished hoeing a few rows of potatoes. Dad hadn't said how many rows, so I asked him, and he said, "Let your conscience be your guide. But there are several that ought to be done."

My conscience wasn't sure how to be a guide to a boy that didn't like to hoe potatoes. So I thought I ought to know exactly how many "several" was and maybe that would help. As soon as Dad and Mom and Charlotte Ann had gone, I looked up the word in our brand-new dictionary, and it said, "Indefinite: more than one or two, but not many." The only thing was, I forgot and left the dictionary open right where I had been looking, and when Dad came home later, he found out what I had done and —but that's getting ahead of the story.

Anyway, just to be sure I'd hoed several, I actually hoed three, which was more than one or two but wasn't many.

Then I had left my hoe in the shade, leaning it up against one of the big pignut trees at the end of the garden, and had started down the dusty path toward the stile, over which I was going to climb and then hurry as fast as I could to Poetry's house. That's when I had run into the snake on that dry, sunny path.

Whenever Big Jim called a meeting and wanted it in a hurry, we all tried to get there as quick as we could. So when Poetry told me about the gang meeting, we decided to go right away.

"What kind of a snake is it?" Poetry asked.

I said, "I don't know, but maybe Dad will know. He knows pretty near everything there is to know about snakes and birds and toads and fish and things."

"My pop does too," Poetry said.

And even though I knew that my dad knew more than Poetry's dad any day, I didn't say so.

We started to go back up the path toward the pignut trees and our garden. In a little while we'd be going past our house with its big green ivy that covers nearly all the south side—it had just a little open space upstairs where my bedroom window is—and also past another iron pitcher pump at the end of a board walk about twenty feet from our back door. Then we'd go on past the mailbox at the side of the road that says on it "Theodore Collins," which is my dad's name. And then we'd swish across that dusty gravel road and vault over a rail fence. Once in the woods, we'd start running, and quicker than a jackrabbit could do it, we'd be at the spring where the gang was going to meet.

Poetry, being as sure as I was that the snake was dead, did what lots of boys do to dead snakes. He picked it up by the tail and dragged it along behind him till we got to the pignut tree. Then he draped it over the rail fence at the edge of our garden, and we left it there till Dad should get home in the late afternoon. I was going to show it to him and ask him what kind of a snake a boy could scare to death with just his voice or by missing him with a big clod of dirt.

We stopped to look at the snake, hanging there with its head on one side and its tail on the other, and it really looked BIG—almost as long as Little Jim is tall. Little Jim was the littlest member of the Sugar Creek Gang, a super guy with brown curls on the top of his round head, and blue eyes, and a very serious face, though sometimes his face was mischievous.

All of a sudden Poetry looked at our garden and said, "You been hoeing potatoes this afternoon?"

"Sure," I said, half proud of myself.

"It's hard to believe," Poetry said and ducked to get out of the way of my flying fist, which I wouldn't have hit him hard with, since he was my almost best friend.

"Well, I'm surprised," he said.

But it wasn't funny, and I wouldn't laugh.

Just that second there was a heavy, clumsy movement at my feet. Looking down, I saw a big, fat, friendly-looking garden toad, which I had almost stepped on and smashed.

"Hi, Warty," I said down to him.

"Hi, who?" Poetry exclaimed.

"Warty," I said, "Dad's pet toad. He lives here in the garden and eats cutworms and mosquitoes and bugs and stuff. Last night Dad and I made a big supper for him."

"Supper! For a *toad!*" Poetry looked down at Warty, who was sitting as quiet as an old setting hen on a nest, all widened out like a mother chicken covering a nest full of eggs.

"Sure," I said and explained. "Dad hung a sheet over the fence right here, close to where Warty hangs out, and turned his big electric lantern on the sheet for fifteen minutes. And all kinds of bugs and night moths and things flew against it, and those that plopped down to the ground, Warty gobbled up. Look—he's as fat as a stuffed toad today"—which Warty was. I'd never seen him so fat.

When I was littler, Pop had taught me to be very glad if we had a toad living in our garden, because toads are the farmer's friends. "A toad will eat over ten thousand injurious insects in one summer," he had told me.

"Let's see you throw your voice at *him* and kill *him*," Poetry said.

But I wouldn't. Besides, I thought Poetry was just making fun of me.

So he decided to try it himself, which he did, yelling down at Warty in his half-man-half-boy's voice, which is the kind of voice he had, he being at the age in his life when a boy is part boy and part man, like a tadpole about to turn into a frog.

But Warty, who had dived halfway under a

rhubarb leaf, just blinked his lazy-looking eyes at us or at nothing and didn't move a muscle.

Well, we had to hurry on. Just as we reached our henhouse, I turned around to take a final look at the big fierce-looking snake hanging on the garden fence, and it wasn't there!

Poetry looked at the same time and said, "Your dead snake doesn't like hanging on a fence in the hot sun for people to look at, or else he lost his balance and fell off"—which was probably right, I thought.

Anyway, when Dad came home, I could remember where the snake had been hanging, and it'd be as easy as falling off a rail fence to find it lying there in the weeds.

"What's that song you're whistling?" Poetry asked me all of a sudden.

"What song?" I listened to my thoughts, and, sure enough, I had been whistling a song and didn't know it. In a second I remembered what it was. It was one of the hymns we sometimes sing in the Sugar Creek church on Sunday mornings, when Mom and Dad and Charlotte Ann and I are all sitting together in a row. I could hardly believe my astonished thoughts when I realized that it was a song called "A Mighty Fortress," which I remembered was written by a man who, our minister said, was a converted priest named Martin Luther. The place in the song that I had been whistling was where it tells about Satan, and the words were "One little word shall fell him."

I didn't understand it very well, but I could

sort of feel that it was the Savior of the world whose word was strong enough to hit the Devil and knock the living daylights out of him— even if He threw at him only one little word.

Anyway, I felt kind of good inside for some reason.

But it was time to get going to the gang meeting.

"I wonder what Big Jim wants a meeting for?" I asked Poetry, as we decided to run to make up the lost time.

Boy oh boy, if I had known what that gang meeting was going to be about, and also what was going to happen to us before the things we had planned at that meeting were finally all finished, I'd *really* have been excited.

If I had known that, later that year, when summer was over and winter came and there was a lot of snow everywhere, the gang would have to make a very important trip up into the hills to the old haunted house I told you about in the last story of the Sugar Creek Gang—if I had only known . . .

But I didn't, so Poetry and I weren't even excited as we hurried on to the spring where we were to meet the gang.

I can hardly wait till I write that far in the story before telling you about that terribly exciting experience. If we hadn't had Big Jim's rifle along with us, every one of us might have died.

3

Even while Poetry and I were running *lickety-sizzle* through the woods, following the path made by barefoot boys' bare feet—and wondering what on earth could be so important that Big Jim, our leader, had to call a special meeting to tell us about it—I was still thinking about that heavy, four-foot-long snake I had killed all by myself, either by scaring it to death or maybe by a small stone that had been in the clod of dirt I had missed it with.

Dad would be proud of me, I thought, for killing such a big snake, but my grayish-brown-haired mom would probably look at me across the supper table and say, "Let me see your hands. Are you sure you washed them after handling that snake?" It's the kind of question Mom asks me after I've handled almost anything, especially if she wants me to help her with some work in the house. It's the kind of question Little Jim says his mom also asks him maybe twenty times a day.

Poetry, who was puffing along behind me, all of a sudden yelled a breathy yell and said, "Hey! The papaws are turning brown! Look!"

I stopped quick, looked to my right to the thicket of papaw shrubs that grew not more than forty feet from the path—there were several wild gooseberry bushes there also—and, sure enough, Poetry was right. I could see a half-dozen pear-shaped brown papaws half hidden among their long bright-green leaves.

"Let's pick a couple for Circus," Poetry said.

Circus, as you know, is the acrobatic member of our gang. He is the only one of us who likes the taste of papaws better than the rest of us.

We crossed to the papaw thicket, and in a jiffy I had two of the wrinkled, brown-skinned fruits in my hand. Poetry and I right away each were eating one. A papaw is like a banana inside, only softer, and is as soft and yellow as the custard Mom puts in her custard pies. It was so sickeningly sweet that only a bite or two was all I could eat.

There were always one or two or more large, hard seeds in each papaw, which I liked to save and carry around in my pockets, the way a boy likes to carry a buckeye, which is supposed to keep him from getting rheumatism and doesn't. But a boy likes to carry one anyway. I had a buckeye in my pocket right that minute.

All of a sudden Poetry acted as if he didn't like the bite of the custard-soft yellow papaw he had in his mouth. He turned his face the other way, which you are supposed to do when you have to spit, so other people won't see you do it, and I heard him say, sounding as though he had mush in his mouth, "That's the most insipid taste I ever tasted."

"The most *what* kind of taste you ever tasted?" I asked, tasting the same kind of taste myself.

He said, "Insipid."

"Just because you know a hundred poems by heart isn't any reason why you have to use the longest words in the dictionary," I said to him.

Picking another wrinkled-skinned softish papaw, I looked down the hill toward the spring, which was still fifty yards away, and saw Circus himself, halfway up a small sapling that grew there. And down on the ground, looking up at him, was little red-haired Tom Till, the newest member of our gang. So I said to Poetry, "I'll beat you there." I started to run, with him after me.

Well, in only a few more minutes, we were all there: Big Jim, our leader, who is the only one of us who has any fuzz on his upper lip; Circus, our acrobat; Little Jim, the cutest one of us—in fact, the *only* one of us who is cute; Tom Till, who has more freckles and even redder hair than I have; Dragonfly, the spindle-legged and pop-eyed member, who has hay fever and asthma in the summer part of the time; and last of all, myself, red-haired, freckle-faced, fiery-tempered Bill Collins, Theodore Collins's only boy, whom he sometimes tells people is his "first and worst son," not meaning it, exactly.

All of us were sitting or lying down in different directions, the way we generally are at a meeting. When Big Jim got us quiet enough so he could be heard, he said with a very grim face, "I want every one of you to vote yes on the proposition, not because I say so but because, as soon as you hear about it, you'll know you ought to. It's very important."

"Then let's take a 'sight unseen' vote," Dragonfly said, and I noticed his face had an expression on it as if he was getting ready to be allergic to something or other and sneeze. A sight-unseen vote was the kind we sometimes took when we all made up our minds that we'd do whatever Big Jim wanted us to without knowing what it was first.

"How many want a sight-unseen vote?" Big Jim asked.

We all put up our hands except Circus.

Big Jim looked around at all of us, and his eyes stopped at Circus, who had one of my papaws in his hand and was holding it up looking at it as if he was getting ready to take an insipid bite.

"What's the matter, Circus?" Big Jim asked. "Why don't you put your hand up?"

"It is up," Circus said. "S-see," he stammered on purpose. "I've got my p-p-papaw up!"

Little Jim giggled, but it didn't seem very funny, especially because I was a little worried by the expression on Big Jim's face. It seemed to say that we were about to vote on something that was not only important but maybe sad too.

Well, we took a sight-unseen vote, and then Big Jim said, "All right, gang, here's what you've just voted yes to . . ."

While he was starting to tell us, I squirmed myself around into another uncomfortable position behind Poetry's back with my red head looking over the top of him.

"It's this way"—Big Jim's words came out from under his fuzzy mustache—"there's a new boy moved into the neighborhood—"

When he got that far, different ones of us, including me, interrupted disgustedly, exclaiming, "NO!"

That would mean that there'd probably be another boy for one of us to have to lick before he could belong to our gang. Nearly always when a new boy moved into Sugar Creek territory, he was the kind of boy who wanted to run the gang, or wanted to introduce a lot of new ideas, or else he was the kind of dumb person who used swear words, which none of the gang used anymore on account of we'd become Christians, and Christians are supposed to have sense enough to have respect for the One who made them.

Also, nearly every new boy who had come into our neighborhood used all kinds of filthy talk about girls. And if he was a big boy, Big Jim nearly always got into a fight with him and knocked the living daylights out of him, on account of Big Jim's being a special friend of a girl named Sylvia, who was our minister's daughter, and also because all our mothers used to be girls themselves. It made us all boiling mad to hear filthy words said about them, even though,

I'll have to admit, I didn't like girls very well myself on account of . . . well, I just didn't.

So when Big Jim said, "There's a new boy moved into our neighborhood," it meant our gang would be interrupted for a while.

"Don't worry," Big Jim consoled us, "we won't have to lick him. He's a great guy. His dad is going to work for my dad this summer, and his mother will help my mother with the canning and things, and they'll live in the little brown house Dad and I just finished building. We had to have another hired man, and we just happened to get a family with a boy in it."

"That's better than having one with a girl in it," Dragonfly said. He was the only one of us who was more afraid of girls than the rest of us.

But Circus gave him a fierce frown. Circus, as you know, had six sisters, and even though sometimes he had small fights with them, as brothers sometimes do with their sisters, he still liked them and would fight *for* them at the drop of a hat.

"What's he look like? How big is he?" Little Tom Till wanted to know.

And Big Jim said, "He hasn't learned to walk alone yet. You see—"

At that, we all interrupted him with a lot of different exclamations. I got a let-down feeling. Imagine calling a special meeting to talk about a baby boy who was so little he couldn't walk yet!

But then Big Jim explained it to us. "He has what is called cerebral palsy, and he was born that way. Even though he's ten years old, he can't walk without leaning on something or somebody, and part of the time he wheels himself around in a wheelchair. He can't use his hands very well, and sometimes they won't do what he wants them to do at all. But he can talk pretty well when he's not too excited. He's really a good kid, and he reads a lot and wants to learn to do everything. We'll have to take him with us sometimes on our gang trips, and we'll have to act like he is a perfectly normal boy and not tell him we feel sorry for him, and stuff like that. Dad says so."

Well, when one of our parents says so about something, that nearly always settles it for the whole gang.

I was watching Little Jim at the time. His cute mouselike face was always so kind, and I noticed that he had an expression on it that seemed to say he was already sorry for the new boy and pitied him.

"What's his name?" he asked.

And when Big Jim said, "Jimmy Lion," it was time for all of us to gasp and exclaim again. Why, that made *three* Jims in our neighborhood! We had Big Jim, our fuzzy-mustached leader; Little Jim, our littlest member; and now Jimmy Lion!

"How big is he?" Poetry asked.

And when Big Jim said, "Almost halfway between Little Jim and me," Tom Till's high-pitched, soprano voice cut in and said, "Let's call him Middle-sized Jim."

24

We put it to a vote and decided it quicker than anything.

"Is that all we called this meeting for?" I asked. "If it is, I move we adjourn and let's all go in swimming."

"Second the motion," Poetry said. He "thirded" it by beginning to unbutton his shirt and to roll himself into a sitting position so that he could get up quicker.

"Remember," Big Jim said, "we're not to say anything or do anything that will embarrass Middle-sized Jim or make him feel he's different from us, because it would have been very easy for any one of us to have been born that way, if—"

He stopped, not saying what we all knew he was thinking. Boys always do more *thinking* about God than *talking* about Him. But I knew if Big Jim had finished what he had started to say, he would have said, "It would have been easy for any one of us to have been born handicapped, if God, who is the Ruler of everything, had let us be."

Deep down inside of me, I was thankful I had a good strong body that would do most everything I wanted it to, although sometimes my parents had a hard time getting my hands and feet to do what *they* wanted them to do.

Pretty soon we were on our way to the old swimming hole, where, I knew, we'd have the time of our lives. I felt kind of sad inside, though, on account of the new boy who couldn't walk, so I slowed down and let the gang run on ahead.

I was imagining, *What if I couldn't run—in fact, couldn't even walk?* I looked out toward old Sugar Creek, my very best nature friend, who was making a very happy little rippling sound about twenty feet from me. There was some fast, sparkling, clear water tumbling over the rocks close to the shore. I stood there listening to it, looking at the hundreds of sparkles in it, feeling good and sad at the same time.

I didn't know Little Jim had stopped too, until I heard him sigh behind me.

In case you haven't read any of the other Sugar Creek Gang stories yet, and don't know how that little guy is always thinking out loud and saying things that my dad calls "philosophical," I'd better tell you that almost anytime you can expect that kind of thought to come tumbling out of his cherry-shaped mouth.

Anyway, while Little Jim and I were standing side by each, looking at and listening to the happy water with maybe a thousand sparkles in it, he piped up and said, "It's nice to have stars in the daytime too." Then all of a sudden, he noticed the rest of the gang laughing and splashing farther up the creek, and away he went, with me chasing right after him.

4

The first time I met Middle-sized Jim was that very afternoon. I had to go over to his house to take a pie, which, by the time we got through swimming, Mom had got home and baked. Different ones of the Sugar Creek Gang's mothers had decided to make the Lion family welcome to Sugar Creek by taking them some homemade baked goods. Mom had baked a very nice-smelling raspberry pie, which is my favorite, and wrapped it up in waxed paper.

I put it in the wire basket on the handle bars of my bicycle, and pretty soon I was pedaling like everything toward Big Jim's house, which was across the road from Circus's house, where all of Circus's awkward sisters lived. One of them, named Lucille, who was about my size, was not as awkward as the rest and would smile back at me across the schoolroom sometimes.

When I got past Circus's house, I turned right, went down a narrow county road, and pretty soon came to the new brown house Big Jim's dad had made for the Lions to live in.

It was a pretty little house, I thought. As I put on my brakes and stopped out in front and leaned my bike up against a maple tree that grew there, I noticed a new tin mailbox with the name "John Lion" on it, which I guessed was Middle-sized Jim's pop's name.

Then I saw Jim himself, sitting in a wheel-chair with some kind of swinging folding table beside him with a typewriter on it. He was using one of his very awkward-looking hands to hit the different typewriter keys. He hadn't seen me come up or heard me, either, I guess.

I didn't know what to say or how to say it, but I remembered our sight-unseen vote, so I stood there looking at him as politely as I could. It seemed there wasn't a thing to say to a boy I didn't know and who had cerebral palsy. I noticed the braces on his legs. Also there was a pair of crutches close beside him, leaning against the porch railing.

Well, I took the wrapped-up pie in my hands, feeling how warm it was and knowing how good it would taste on account of I had helped our family eat maybe five hundred pies like that since I was born a red-haired baby boy. Without knowing I was going to do it, I cleared my throat.

Middle-sized Jim heard me, stopped doing what he had awkwardly been doing, and looked me right square in my greenish-gray eyes with a pair just as greenish-gray as mine. And he said, with his neck jerking a little and leaning toward the left, "I'm sorry. I didn't see you." He raised his kind of friendly voice and called, "Mother! We have company!" Then his eyes looked out toward the tree where my bike was, and he said, "I'm going to learn to ride a bike sometime. I've earned almost enough money to buy one."

Just like that, I thought. It was easy to get acquainted with him. He didn't act bashful or embarrassed, but I thought, *How in the world can he learn to ride a bicycle?*

"I have to learn to walk first," he said.

Well, we talked a little while about different things, and pretty soon I was on my way home with the last thing he had said tumbling around in my mind, which was, "Any time you need any letters typed, bring them over, and I'll type them for you for free. I have a big library of books, too. Books on nature especially—flowers and trees and birds and all kinds of animals and reptiles such as snakes and turtles. Anything you want to know about."

I decided that if Dad didn't know what kind of snake I'd killed that afternoon, maybe Middle-sized Jim could look it up for me in one of his nature books.

When I came pedaling up to "Theodore Collins" on our mailbox, I could see my reddish-brown-mustached, bushy-eyebrowed dad in our garden by the twin pignut trees. He had a hoe in his hands and was hoeing like a house afire.

I wanted, the worst way, to swing happily into the drive, lean my bike up against the side of our toolshed, which is beside the grape arbor, and yell out to him about the big snake I'd killed. Then I'd go dashing over and show it to him, lying there in the weeds beside the rail fence. But for some reason, I was thinking about the dictionary definition of "several," which was "more than one or two, but not many."

Knowing that Dad had probably hoed several rows of potatoes himself, and *his* several would not only be more than one or two but maybe five or six, I decided to go out to the barn and start to gather the eggs. That is, I decided, and then right away I undecided it.

When my dad called to me in a gruff voice, saying, "WILLIAM!" I knew there was something I had done wrong or that I hadn't done right or just hadn't done and should have, because that is the only time he ever calls me *William.*

"What?" I yelled back as cheerfully as I could. "I'm going to gather the eggs!"

"Come here!" Dad's voice sounded as if he meant business, so I denied myself the privilege of gathering the eggs. Not wanting him to think I was worried about the several rows of potatoes that were left unhoed, I started to whistle and also to sing a little. In fact, the tune was the one about "one little word shall fell him."

"Hurry up!" he called, and I hurried a little.

Dad leaned on his hoe till I got to the garden fence, then he said, "You like our new dictionary, Bill?"

I felt myself blushing all the way up to the roots of my red hair. Had he guessed what word I had looked up, and was he going to give me a scolding?

"You left the dictionary open," he said. "You should never leave a good book open on a windy, dusty afternoon like it was today." Then just as though he wanted to change the subject, he said, "What else did you do today?"

I breathed a sigh of wonderful relief and said cheerfully, "I killed a great big, ugly, heavy-bodied snake. I don't know what kind it is. I never saw such a fierce snake in my life. He's lying dead there in the weeds right behind you."

Right away, I was in the garden with Dad, and he and I were looking around in the weeds below the place where Poetry had draped the snake over the fence. But the big, fierce-looking dead snake wasn't there anywhere!

"That's funny," I said, puzzled.

"What did he look like?" Dad asked me, holding his hoe in both hands as though he was ready to cut a snake in two if he saw one that was alive.

When I told him it was reddish-yellow with brown blotches on it and that it puffed out its neck fiercely and struck at me and hissed and that its nose was turned up like a scoop shovel, his bushy eyebrows went down, and he looked serious. "Where did you say he was when you first saw him?"

"Lying in the path, halfway between here and the stile—all by himself."

"And were you all by yourself, without a thing with which to protect yourself?" Dad's voice was anxious.

"Except for a clod of dirt as big around as Charlotte Ann's head, which I missed him with when I threw it at him. But I threw my voice at him, too, and that killed him. Scared him to death," I said. "The very minute the clod struck close to his three-inch-wide head and puffed-out neck, he twisted himself up into several knots, plopped over on his back, and died. Poetry came along just then, and we poked at him with a stick to see if he was really dead, and he was. Poetry picked him up by the tail then and draped him over the fence right here."

"Sounds like a fish story," Dad said. "You're sure you're not kidding me?"

"It's the truth," I said, still looking for the greenish-yellow-stomached snake.

"You say he puffed out his neck and head and hissed at you?"

"Yes sir."

Pop's face looked as if he believed me, then he said, "Sounds like a hissing adder or a puff adder. If it was, you're lucky to be alive, Bill Collins."

At that, he looked around very carefully to see if he could still find it, but he couldn't.

We did find Warty, though, who had been hiding in the shade of a very large plantain leaf.

When Dad saw him, he said, "Well, hello, Warty! Glad to see you're still alive, anyway."

I noticed he'd called both Warty and me by the names he liked us by, and I felt better but was still kind of tense inside. Where, I thought, was the hissing adder now?

Just that second there was the sound of chickens making about a hundred scared squawks in our chicken yard. I looked up in time to see a big hawk swooping down from the top of one of the pignut trees. He made a dive straight for a little lonely, fluffy, peeping chicken by the grape arbor. And the next thing I knew, the hawk was up in the air again, and the soft, fluffy baby chick was gone.

"That's what happened to your snake," Dad said. "Chicken hawks like snakes too."

And maybe he was right. In fact I knew he was—until the next day when I was finishing hoeing several more rows of potatoes.

This time my *several* was not only more than one or two; it seemed it was more than *many*.

Poetry was there too. He had stopped at the Lions' den, as Middle-sized Jim called their house, and wheeled him over in his wheelchair, and Middle-sized Jim had showed us how he could almost walk without his crutches.

But every time after he had taken a few steps, he fell *ker-sprawlety-plop*. While we were helping him up, he'd say, "It didn't hurt a bit. I'm used to it," and he would be grinning as though he was having fun.

We told him the snake story. "A great big chicken hawk ate him up," I said.

But Middle-sized Jim spoiled our story for us by saying, "Chicken hawks won't eat dead things unless they kill them themselves."

I looked up from my hoeing, and I thought he had a mischievous grin on his face, although

I couldn't tell for sure on account of his smiling almost all the time anyway.

Well, after what seemed a terribly long time, I finished hoeing the last row, and since we were all thirsty we decided to go down to the stile to get a drink at the iron pitcher pump there, rather than at the pump at the end of the board walk near our house.

Middle-sized Jim could make it OK with his crutches, and several times he took a couple of steps by himself before losing his balance and falling and landing all tangled up in the dust of the path. But he'd always just laugh, and we'd help him up and go on. And then, all of a sudden he let out a yell. "Look! There's your dead snake taking a sunbath!"

I looked, and what to my wondering eyes should appear but a reddish-yellow snake as big as the one I had killed yesterday.

5

A boy has a hard time believing his eyes when the mind under his red hair tells him that what he sees isn't so. Yesterday we'd picked up a dead snake and carried it to the rail fence that enclosed our garden and had draped it over the top rail and left it. A chicken hawk had eaten it. But today—twenty-four hours later—here it was, the same big, heavy-bodied, savage-looking snake, lying alive out in the middle of the field!

We were already close to it, and just as it had done yesterday, it acted as mad as anything. It was puffing out its neck and head and hissing and striking in our direction as though it wanted to kill us quick and would if we came any closer.

"He's mad because we woke him up out of his sleep," Poetry said.

"We interrupted his sunbath, and he probably wanted privacy," Middle-sized Jim said.

I had a big stick with me this time, and I was going to be sure we really killed it. I started to make a rush at the snake and take a swipe at its upraised head.

But Middle-sized Jim's excited voice stopped me, saying, "Don't, Bill! Wait! I've got an idea! That's probably a brother or a wife of the one you killed yesterday! Let's see if you can scare *this* one to death!"

I looked at his grinning face but couldn't tell whether he was making fun of me or not. He was having a little trouble balancing himself with his crutches, so I made a dive in his direction to keep him from falling, just as Poetry said, "Let's see what *my* voice will do."

Without waiting for us to let him, Poetry picked up a big clod like the one I'd had yesterday and squashed it into a thousand pieces of dirt and dust about a foot from the snake's hissing head. He yelled down at it fiercely, making up a poem at the same time, saying:

"You great big ugly squirming lummox,
  Get over on your back and turn up your
    stomach!"

Well, you can believe it or not, but just like the snake I'd done that to yesterday, that reddish-yellow, brown-splotched snake all of a sudden went into contortions like a boy having a spasm from eating too many green apples or green grapes. The next thing we knew, there it was, over on its back with its pretty greenish-yellow stomach shining in the sun, and it wasn't even moving a muscle! Imagine that!

That made Middle-sized Jim laugh. "I knew it. I knew it!" he exclaimed. "It's a hognose snake! That's the way they do when they're cornered. First, they act very fierce, like they are the most dangerous snake in the world, and try

drink out of the same cup on account of it might spread different kinds of diseases.

All of an excited sudden, Middle-sized Jim let out a yell and said, "Look! There he goes! See him? He's heading back to the garden!"

Poetry stopped pumping. I dropped my cup of water and grabbed up my stick. This time there was going to be a dead snake for sure. As fast as I could, with Poetry at my heels, I dashed back across the bare field.

I never saw a snake run so fast in my life— glide, rather, which is the way snakes move. Boy, it was really going!

"Hurry up!" I yelled over my shoulder at Poetry, and he came puffing after me at a very noisy, dusty rate. I hoped I could make it before the snake got to the pignut trees and lost itself in the weeds by the rail fence where we couldn't find it.

And then the queerest thing happened. It was so interesting and exciting and also so astonishing that it almost made me forget the snake.

From behind me, I heard Middle-sized Jim's voice yelling, "Hey, you guys! Don't kill him! Let him live!"

I looked back over my shoulder, and there was our new friend, who hadn't walked five feet in his life without holding onto someone or something, and he was running after us, drag- ging his crutches! Running! A boy who couldn't even walk was *running!* It didn't make sense. He wasn't running straight, the way the members of our gang did, but he was running almost as fast as Poetry and I.

I took my eyes off the snake for a second, and so did Poetry, and I yelled back to Middle-sized Jim. "Hey," I said, "you're running!"

Then I wished I hadn't said it, for the minute Middle-sized Jim heard me, he got a queer expression on his face as if he had just lost something that was worth a million dollars. And the next thing I knew, he was struggling to keep his balance. A second later, down he went, *ker-sprawlety-plop* onto the ground, stirring up a cloud of dust, which the wind picked up and blew across the field toward the stile, like powdered snow blowing across the field in the wintertime.

Well, that was the first time Middle-sized Jim ever really walked, and he had not only walked but he had run. He was so pleased with himself, he could hardly believe it.

We were so excited that we let our snake get away, and we never saw it again until two weeks later when it turned up in the most interesting way you could ever imagine.

First, though, I'd better explain that Middle-sized Jim's doctor said that he had learned to walk—or rather *run*—because he had got what is called "absolute concentration." He got it when he saw the snake getting away and Poetry and me trying to catch it. He had wanted to stop us from killing it because he knew it wasn't a dangerous snake, and he had forgotten all about his not being able to run. Seeing *us* run, he had been so excited that he ran himself.

His running wasn't like any ordinary boy's. It was half-run and half-lurch. But he could do it without his crutches, which was wonderful.

That was the beginning of a much happier life for Middle-sized Jim. Also it happened to be the very thing that makes this the story of the most exciting adventure we'd had in a long time, which, pretty soon, I'll tell you about.

Before I do, I'll have to tell you where we found old Hognose again, and what he was doing, and why. I'll also have to tell you a little more about Warty, my dad's favorite toad friend, and his own very exciting adventure.

I guess I didn't realize that hognose snakes and garter snakes would rather eat a toad for supper than a boy would like to eat a plateful of raw-fried potatoes and bread and butter when he is hungry. But they would. Only, as I said, I didn't realize it. And, of course, I didn't know that snake had been hanging around our garden on purpose because he had his appetite set on making a delicious supper out of Warty.

Warty must have guessed that old Hognose was laying for him, because one day he disappeared, and we didn't see him around the garden for maybe a week. And there were all kinds of cutworms that kept snipping off Mom's baby beans and sugar-corn shoots, and there didn't seem to be much we could do to stop them.

"Maybe Warty finds all the cutworms he can

stuff himself with out in the cornfield," Mom said one day, and maybe she was right.

Anyway, several days later—one or two but not many—I was coming home from fishing down in the branch with Dragonfly. On the way back, I was halfway through one of our other potato patches, which is quite a ways from our regular garden, when I was startled by a clumsy movement at my feet. Looking down, I saw a large, lazy-looking brown toad in the skimpy shade of a wild carrot, which somebody's boy should have pulled long ago.

The wild carrot, or Queen Anne's lace, which is one of its other names, was Dad's worst-hated weed. Mom liked to look at its pretty lacelike flowers, which, when they are only half opened, are all in a little circle with a hollow in the middle. And that's the reason it is sometimes called by still another name, Bird's Nest. But Dad always made me pull up all the Queen Anne's lace I could find on account of its being a very bad weed with very stubborn roots, he says, and if you leave one for a year, then next year there'll be a great big family of them to get rid of.

As soon as I saw Dad's toad friend, I cheerfully said down to him, "Why, hello, Warty, old pal! Am I glad to see you! Will Mom ever be pleased!"

I decided to run and tell Mom about him right away, so I started to the house. Then I changed my mind, because an interesting plan popped into my head. In a jiffy, I had Warty picked up in the big handkerchief I had in my pocket, not exactly wanting to handle him with my bare hands.

Right under a toad's warty skin there are glands that give off a bitter fluid of some kind that is just a little bit poisonous. If a dumb puppy tries to pick up a toad to play with it, he quick drops it, not liking the toad's taste. I was afraid Warty wouldn't know I was a friend and that I'd maybe get some poisonous gland fluid on my bare hands.

Some boys think toads cause warts on a boy's hands, but they don't. It makes Dad mad to hear anybody say that about an innocent toad, because it isn't so at all.

Anyway, I wrapped up Warty in my handkerchief, leaving his nose out so he could breathe. Holding him tight so that he wouldn't squirm himself out of my grasp, I carried him back to the garden where Mom's cabbage plants needed him to take care of them.

To be sure Warty wouldn't hop away again, I tied the end of my fishing line around the joint of one of his fat legs, leaving the rest of the long line on the reel on my fishing pole. Warty would be free to hop all over the garden and gobble up all the cutworms he could find that night—for as you maybe know, cutworms always do their cutting off of cabbage plants and young corn shoots at night.

It was sort of like tethering out our old one-eared cow on a long rope where she can eat grass in every direction for quite a long ways, but she can't get away to eat where she is not supposed to.

"There you are, my friend," I said to Warty, as soon as I had him tied to the end of the line. "Now see to it that you behave yourself and stay here where we need you a lot worse than we do down yonder in that other potato patch."

Mom certainly was pleased when I told her Warty was back again and that I'd brought him myself. I didn't tell her about tying him up.

At the supper table that night, Dad and Mom and Charlotte Ann and I sat very quiet for a minute as we always do before we eat, with our heads bowed while Dad asked the blessing. For a second or so I opened my eyes and looked at Mom's kind of grayish-brown hair, all combed nice and pretty, the way she hurries up and combs it whenever she knows my dad is coming home from working in the field.

I also noticed his reddish-brown hair and his long, shaggy, reddish-brown eyebrows, which he also combs sometimes and won't let the barber clip them shorter, the way barbers try to do, Dad says, if you don't stop them.

Also I saw my brown-haired baby sister's head. I noticed she had her hands unfolded, and her eyes wide open, and she was looking around at different things. Without knowing I was going to do it, I whispered to her, saying, "*Sh!* Charlotte Ann! Shut your eyes! Dad is going to ask the blessing! You're supposed to have your eyes shut!"

My dad probably heard me, but he didn't

pay any attention to me. In his prayer he said that we were thankful for the food before us, which I certainly was because it was raw-fried potatoes, bread and butter, apple pie and cheese, and some leftover cold chicken.

There was also a bottle of cod-liver oil from which Mom was going to put half a spoonful into Charlotte Ann's orange juice as soon as Pop finished praying. In fact, right that second, Charlotte Ann was stretching one hand as far as she could toward the glass of juice—the way maybe Warty, that very minute, was straining at the end of my fishing line for a nice juicy cutworm.

Pop's prayer was kind of short, as it sometimes is at supper time, when he knows all of us are hungry and tired. But I remember he prayed for Middle-sized Jim, saying, "Dear Father, we pray that You will bless all the fine boys and girls in the world who were born like Jimmy Lion. Help people to understand them and to love them. We thank You for the blessing Jimmy has been to all of us with his sunny disposition and his eager mind. Help us all to apply ourselves to our studies as earnestly as he does . . ."

When my dad got that far, I thought maybe he was praying for me too, and I couldn't tell for sure whether he was talking to God or to me. But it seemed maybe I ought to study a little harder that fall when school started.

Mom, hearing him pray for Jimmy, must have been reminded of the hognose snake that had disappeared a week or two ago. And that must have reminded her of my hands, because the very second Dad finished his prayer, she looked straight at my hands, which were already busy spreading butter on a slice of her home-made bread.

I quick spoke up and said, just to show her I knew what she was thinking about, "I didn't touch Warty at all. I used my handkerchief."

Then I saw Mom's face get a strange expression on it, and I knew I'd made a mistake even before she said, "You mean you used one of your nice white handkerchiefs to pick up a dirty toad!"

I had to quick think of something to defend myself with, so I said, "It wasn't *all* white. It already had bloodstains on it from trying to—"

"Blood!" Mom said, astonished.

"I—yes, ma'am," I said, unusually polite. "Dragonfly and I were wading in the branch, and he stepped on a sharp stone and cut his foot, and I had to help him stop it from bleeding."

"You were wading in the *branch!*" my dad said with an exclamation point in his voice. He looked around the edge of the table at my overalls to see if, when I'd had them rolled up and was in the water, the trouser legs had come down as they sometimes do and had gotten wet.

"We didn't have our overalls *on*," I said. "It was too deep there."

"What?" Dad asked. "The only place the branch is deep is down near where it empties into the creek, and that's close to the road! I hope you boys didn't wade out there *that* close to the road with your clothes off!"

"We had to," I said. "We were looking for something we had lost."

"You lost something? *Bill Collins!*" Mom said. "You haven't lost anything important, I hope!"

"Just a piece of fishing line that got fastened onto the bottom on a snag."

"Did you have to break your new line?" Dad asked.

And I said, yawning, as if it didn't matter much, "Oh, a few feet, maybe."

"Several?" Dad asked. Out of the corner of my eye, as I poked into my mouth a forkful of great-tasting raw-fried potatoes, I saw that he had a twinkle in his eyes, and I knew he wasn't mad at me at all for having hoed only three rows of potatoes that other afternoon.

"I'll try to make it six or seven next time," I said to him.

And Mom said, "You mean you'll try to lose more line next time?"

My dad looked at me and winked, and I made up my mind that the very next time I had to hoe several rows of potatoes, I'd see if I could stretch the word "several" until it was almost as long as "many."

When I was in my room that night with the light out and was getting ready to drop into bed on the nice clean sheets Mom had put on that very day, I looked out the window to the moonlit garden where Warty was tethered. I was a little worried about him, wondering if he would get himself tangled up in the line before he even got started on his trips up and down the corn rows for cutworms.

Warty really knew how to gobble them up too, just as he does a fly or a mosquito or a grub or anything else in the insect family that gets within two inches of his mouth. Warty's tongue isn't fastened at the *back* of his mouth as mine is but at the *front,* and he can all of a sudden flip his tongue out like a whip. If there is a fly buzzing around his head, quicker than nothing there isn't any fly, and the only way you know Warty got him is when you see the tiny movement he makes in his throat when he swallows.

Once Dad and I watched Warty hopping down one of Mom's bean rows, and even though we didn't see his long sticky whiplike tongue catch a single bug, when he got to the end of the row, there wasn't a one left.

As I said, I was looking out the window toward our moonlit garden. I cocked one ear in Warty's direction to see if I could hear my reel clicking, the way it does when I'm fishing and get a bite. But as hard as I listened, I couldn't hear a thing except the leaves of the ivy vine that grew across the upper part of the window, rustling in the wind.

So I quick dropped down on my knees to pray a sort of tired prayer to the heavenly

Father, whom my parents had taught me to pray to when I was as little as Charlotte Ann, and I've been doing it ever since. I was so tired I couldn't think straight. Maybe my words were mixed up a little, but even though God might be pretty busy running such a big world and a whole skyful of stars and planets and things, still I just sort of knew that He liked boys and was interested in the things they like to do. It also seemed He even liked me, Bill Collins, and that He wasn't holding it against me for praying such an ordinary prayer.

I guess I must have gotten Dad's supper-time prayer mixed up with mine, although I wasn't sure, but I heard myself saying, "Bless Middle-sized Jim and take care of him. He's been a blessing to all of us."

I don't remember finishing my prayer at all, but when I woke up sometime in the middle of the night, I was in bed, so I must have climbed in. I had been dreaming that I was fishing and had hooked a terribly big fish like the kind the gang sometimes catches on our northern fishing trips. In my dream, the reel was singing and singing, and the line was running out clear to the end, and I was trying to hold onto the pole and not lose my fish. That was when I woke up. And then I was sure I had heard a noise out in the garden.

I lay quiet for a minute, my heart pounding. I rolled over to sit on the edge of the bed, leaned forward to the open window, and then I *knew* I was hearing something. I was hearing my reel make little sharp jerking sounds as though the line was being unwound only a little at a time.

Then I grinned to myself there in the moonlight as in my mind's eye I saw Warty hopping down a row of Mom's young cabbage plants with his lightning-quick, sticky tongue flipping in and out, gobbling up cutworms and other plant enemies.

I sighed happily and went back to sleep until morning. Then, just as I do when there is something very interesting to get up for, I sprang out of bed, shoved myself into my clothes and, two steps at a time, was on my way downstairs to see how much of my fishing line had been unwound and if Warty had worked himself loose and run away again.

6

I forgot that I was up earlier than Mom herself and even Dad *him*self. Certainly I was up before Charlotte Ann was supposed to be. So when I heard the screen door slam behind me as I dashed out past our iron pitcher pump, I realized that the loud noise the door had made would probably wake up Charlotte Ann. And once *she* waked up in the morning, that was the end of it for any sleep any of the rest of the family wanted to get.

But it was too late now to go back to shut the door "like a gentleman," as my parents tell me is the way to do it, so I ran on till I came to within about ten feet of the rail fence. Not knowing what to expect, I crept forward quietly till I got to where I could see my fishing pole.

The first thing I noticed was that the reel was nearly all unwound, so I figured Warty must have done quite a lot of traveling. I peeked through the fence, let my eyes run down the length of the line, which had threaded its way around through the potatoes and corn and beans and cabbage plants. Away over at the other side of the garden, not far from the pignut trees, it disappeared in the tall weeds.

What would Warty be doing out there in the weeds? I wondered. It wasn't hot enough for him to be looking for shade, because the sun wasn't even up yet, it was so early.

After climbing over the fence, I followed the trail of the line until I came to where it disappeared. I wondered if Warty had got tangled up in the weeds or what. And then, all of a sudden, in a little open space in the weeds, I saw something that made me stop stock-still and stare. I saw a great big hognose snake fastened onto my line instead of Warty. In fact, the line was right in his mouth! *What on earth!* I thought.

And then, all of a sickening sudden, I knew what had happened. I knew, because I saw a pair of toad's legs sticking out of the snake's mouth. The legs were kicking, making the snake look as if he had two big live horns on his head. That fierce-looking hognose had swallowed my friend Warty headfirst, all the way down to his legs!

I must have gotten there more quietly than I thought, because the snake didn't even seem to realize I was watching him. He kept struggling and struggling with Warty, his head and neck puffed out much farther than they had been the day I'd first seen him and he had been hissing at me.

Warty still hadn't given up, or those two legs wouldn't have been kicking and squirming, and I knew he was trying to back out. The snake's mouth kept working and working. It seemed he was trying to pull Warty in, as if his body was a gunnysack and he was working the end of the sack up around Warty's fat sides.

I was so surprised and also so horrified at what I knew was happening—realizing that maybe I was to blame for tying Warty up so that he couldn't get away—that it was like I was paralyzed. I couldn't even scream for Dad to come to see if he could still save Warty.

And then, the next thing I knew, there was a sort of walking movement in the snake's neck, and Warty's two legs disappeared. And down below the snake's head, I saw a big bulge, which meant that our friendly garden toad was completely swallowed.

Well, I knew there wasn't any use getting hold of my fishing line and trying to pull Warty out. Middle-sized Jim had told me that snakes' teeth are slanted back into their mouths and throats, and I could never pull Warty out.

And then, I got an idea. If Warty wasn't dead yet, and if his tough toad skin had only been scratched by the snake's sharp teeth, he might still be alive. And that idea quick brought me to life.

If you have read some of the other Sugar Creek Gang stories, you know that I had already made up my mind I was going to be a doctor someday and give people medicine to make them well. I would also operate on people. As quick as I got my idea, I raced across the garden, vaulted over the fence, and made a wild dive for the toolhouse, where we kept our hoes and spades.

I was going to quick grab up a hoe and race madly back to the garden, which Warty out of his kind heart had been looking after for us. I was going to get to Warty before old Hognose had a chance to start digesting him, slice the snake in two right close to the place where Warty was, and see if I could get Warty out, still alive. I would use the hoe to chop the snake in two and my Scout knife to do any other operating on him I had to do to get Warty out.

Just as I came out of the toolshed with the hoe, Dad came out of our house's back door, saw me, and exclaimed with irony in his voice, "Well, what do you know!" He must have been astonished. He also must have felt mischievous, because he said to me, "Of all things! Bill Collins has gotten ambitious!"—which is a word to describe people who think of doing things without being told to and who also maybe like to work.

But I couldn't be bothered with anything funny. "Quick!" I yelled to him. "Follow me and help me save Warty's life! He's gotten himself swallowed by a snake!"

A lot of our chickens must have thought that so much noisy excitement close to the house meant something for them to eat. A whole flock of maybe forty hens came rushing toward us, half running and half flying, the way they sometimes do when Mom comes out the kitchen door with a panful of something she's going to toss out to them.

Anyway, when I quick headed back to the garden, yelling for Dad to follow me, I stumbled over a couple of excited hens, one of them being old Bent Comb, who lays her eggs in the haymow. Those two hens and the rest of the chickens went scattering in every main direction there is and also in all the other little directions there are in between, making a noisy scared path for me to run through on my way back to Warty.

"Hurry up!" I yelled back to Dad over my shoulder. At the garden, I vaulted over the fence and swished through the dusty garden as quick as I could without stepping on any corn or cabbages.

When I got there, I found out that my dad had not only followed me, but he had also used his head and had stopped at Mom's clothesline and brought with him the forked stick that we used as a clothesline prop. In less time than I can write it for you, Dad and I went into action.

Maybe I'd better tell you that one time the year before, Dad and our doctor had let me watch a boy having his appendix cut out. So even while I was scared and excited and worried about Warty, I imagined myself to be a doctor, and I gave quick orders to Dad like a doctor giving them to his nurse.

I was holding onto my fishing line so that old Hognose couldn't get away. "Quick!" I said. "Get that forked clothesline prop down on his neck! Pin him to the ground! There—just above the bulge Warty makes!"

And Dad did.

But that snake's head being pinned to the ground made the tail and the rest of his ugly heavy body come to the most excited life you ever saw. It seemed he was trying to twist himself into and out of a million twists and wiggles and knots.

I don't know how I ever did what I did, but I did—and I certainly wasn't smart enough to think that fast either—but suddenly I was standing on the body of the snake with my right foot and was ready to begin my first surgical operation.

"Hey," Dad said, trying to be mischievous at a very serious time. "You can't perform an operation without first giving the patient an anesthetic" (which any boy knows is a medicine a doctor uses on a patient before he operates, so as to kill the pain).

I didn't pay any attention to Dad's half-funny remark. I had my official Scout knife out of my pocket and was opening its sharp cutting blade.

"Aren't you going to kill the pain first?" Pop asked, still with a mischievous grin in his voice.

"I'm going to kill the *snake*," I said.

With my left hand, I grabbed the snake's heavy body halfway between my foot and Warty's bulge and started to operate just as Dad said, "All good doctors wash their hands with soap before they perform an operation."

I couldn't be bothered. All I could think of was my friend Warty inside that bulge, where he couldn't get a breath of fresh air. So I said, "This good doctor will wash his hands *after* the operation."

"Your mother will see to that," my dad remarked.

I was down on my left knee in the garden dirt, my right foot still on the snake's body.

"Never mind making a fancy incision," Pop said. "Just cut him in two and let Warty hop out by himself."

Well, the rest of the operation isn't very pleasant to write about, so I won't write about it. Besides, it was too sad.

"Poor Warty," Dad said after it was all over and Warty lay motionless on the ground. It looked as if he was completely dead. I looked down at him and felt my eyes stinging. I knew that if I had been a little younger, I'd maybe have cried.

"It's all my fault," I said, feeling very sad. "If I hadn't tied him up, he could have gotten away."

"Maybe not," Dad said. "Snakes like that live on toads and frogs—toads especially—and they know how to catch them without help."

I cut my line off, and Dad dug a hole in the corner of the garden for Warty's grave, and there we buried him.

We dug another grave for the snake and covered them both up.

Dad and I were getting to be better and better friends, I thought, as we carried the hoe back toward the toolshed. He was not only my great big dad, who was my mom's husband, but he was a pretty nice person also, even if he was a father.

Just then Mom opened the back door of our house and stood in the doorway and looked at us with a question mark in her eyes. "*Now* what have you two boys been up to?" she asked.

"Bill just performed a surgical operation," Dad said and added, "but the patient died."

"We just had a funeral," I said.

"A funeral?"

"Warty," I said.

We told Mom everything, and her eyes took on a faraway expression. I thought I saw tears in them, but she changed the subject by saying, "If the doctor and the undertaker will get washed up, we'll have breakfast in just a few minutes," which we did.

Well, that was the end of this part of the story and the end also of both the toad and the snake. It was too terribly bad that Warty had to die, I thought. Still, it was a good thing there had been a big hognose snake around our garden, because it was when Middle-sized Jim got excited that time when the snake had been trying to glide away that he had got what his doctor called "absolute concentration" and had learned to walk and even to run. From then on, he could do both, although, as I said, his run was more of a lurch than a run.

Also, it was Middle-sized Jim's learning to walk and run that made the most important part of this story happen. I'll get going on that just as soon as I can.

First, though, I have to tell you about what

happened in our garden the next day when Little Jim came over to our house.

He had come to get a copy of one of Mom's recipes for making a very special kind of pie that Little Jim's mom had tasted at a potluck dinner at their Sunday school class party. I think it was called lemon meringue. Mom had surprised all the other Sugar Creek mothers by mixing in some chopped black walnuts, and it had tasted wonderful.

Little Jim wanted to know the whole story about Warty, just as it happened to Dad and me.

Poetry was already at my house when Little Jim came, and he and I had just finished making a couple of twig whistles and were blowing them, making a lot of boy noise. We took Little Jim out to the garden, and I told the whole story over again, having already told it to Poetry. Little Jim always listened to stories with his face as well as with both ears. His small, mouselike face with its cherry-shaped mouth got a lot of different kinds of expressions on it while he listened.

When I finished, we were all standing near Warty's grave, where Poetry had erected a shingle with a poem on it, which he had written himself:

Here lies Warty, the farmer's best friend.
How sad that he had such a terrible end!

I thought I noticed tears in Little Jim's eyes as he stood looking down at Poetry's poetry.

Then, as he often does when he has a couple of tears that he doesn't want anybody to see, he turned his face away, gave his head a quick toss, and when he looked back again, the tears had disappeared. They had fallen on one of Mom's cabbage plants, maybe. If a cabbage plant could think, it'd probably have been surprised, wondering if it had started to rain saltwater instead of rain.

"Where'd you bury the *snake?*" Little Jim asked.

"Right over there," I said, pointing to a little mound of clay without any marker.

Little Jim walked over to it. Then all of a sudden, he let out a gasp and said, "Hey, you guys! Come here! Look!"

Well, you could have knocked me over with the seedpod of a milkweed when I saw what I saw. About nine inches from Little Jim's brown, bare, dusty feet was a great big, blinking, brown-skinned, warty-looking toad!

Poetry saw it at the same time and exclaimed, "It's Warty! He's come back to life!"

I looked down at the warty-skinned amphibian, which is what Middle-sized Jim says a toad is, and he did look exactly like Warty. He was blinking his glassy eyes as though he was thinking some kind of lazy, mischievous thoughts.

But it just couldn't be Warty, I thought, and said so. "He doesn't have any snake teeth marks on him."

"Maybe they healed up," Little Jim said.

"They couldn't in only one day," Poetry said.

"The only way to know for sure is to dig into his grave to see if he came to life and crawled out," I said.

Dad, hearing all the excitement, came out of the barn.

I saw him and yelled, "Hey, Dad! Come here!"

In a few seconds he was there with us, and we were all standing in a little half circle looking down at the toad's blinking eyes. Dad reached out the toe of his heavy shoe and touched the toad, which right away filled himself up with air, the way toads do, and looked as tight as a toy balloon at a county fair.

"Do you suppose, maybe, *this* one is Warty, instead of the one that got swallowed yesterday?" I asked Dad.

Poetry, feeling extra mischievous that day, made up a new poem real quick and said,

> "His tummy is so round and firm
> Because he ate a fat cutworm."

Pop ignored Poetry's poetry, stooped down, and said in a kind, friendly voice, "Warty, my friend, let's have a look at your left front foot to see if you are you, or if that's you over there under that tombstone," meaning under Poetry's shingle.

When my dad leaned down to Warty and with a small stick tried to get his front foot out where we could see it, all of a sudden that big fat toad gave an acrobatic flip and landed on his back with his brownish stomach exposed to the sky.

"What on *earth!*" I said, remembering that the hognose snake had done the same thing.

Dad ignored my exclamation and said, "Yep, that's Warty! See, there's one toe missing on his left front foot. I accidentally cut it off a week or two ago when I was hoeing several rows of potatoes. The very next day, he disappeared, and I thought that was why he had run away. I thought he didn't like me anymore and wasn't going to oblige the Collins family any longer by eating up our cutworms. I didn't know, of course, that the real reason he ran away was because he was afraid of the snake. Well, well, well, Warty, I won't hurt you. You can get right back on your tummy again."

None of us said anything for a minute, as Dad made us all step back about ten or fifteen feet. "Now keep your eyes on him," he whispered, "and you'll see some acrobatics that will astonish you"—which we did.

Almost right away, I saw first one and then another awkward toad foot straighten out and rise up in the air, and then with a movement that would make any circus acrobat jealous, that toad gave his body a flip, and there he was right side up again.

And that was that. Warty was still alive! *Hurrah!*

I felt sorry for the other toad I had caught, though, and had brought to our garden and tied up, and he had been swallowed by the big, ugly, hognose snake. But our old favorite friend Warty was still alive, and that made me feel fine.

All of a sudden, Little Jim was reminded that he was supposed to hurry home with the copy of Mom's meringue pie recipe. "I've got to get going," he said. "Besides, I haven't practiced my piano lesson yet."

That little guy was certainly a great person, I thought, as I watched him crawl through the rail fence and run as fast as his short legs could carry him toward our front gate—where "Theodore Collins" was on the mailbox beside it—scramble onto his bicycle, and ride away.

I looked up at Dad then. "I'll bet you knew all the time that the toad I was trying to save wasn't Warty. You did, didn't you?"

"I'm afraid I did," he said. "In fact, I was watching you yesterday afternoon while you were tying up your toad with your fishing line. After you had gone to bed last night, I went out to the garden to be sure by taking a look at your toad's toes. I had a little trouble catching him because he was as scared of me as a cottontail rabbit. He started hopping away in short, quick jumps, almost as fast as a frog jumps, unwinding your reel a little with every jump."

And that was that, and a very exciting that, at that.

7

Autumn with a million different shades of color came to Sugar Creek. The hills that year were especially pretty after the first frost. When Mom puts frosting on a cake, it's nearly always one color—white or pink or chocolate brown—but when old Jack Frost gets through with the maples and oaks and elms and sycamores and lindens and a lot of other kinds of trees on the Sugar Creek hills, they have all the colors of the rainbow at the same time.

"Did you ever see such a big bouquet of colors?" I heard Mom say to Dad one day when they were standing out by our barn looking toward Strawberry Hill.

"It is pretty, isn't it?" he answered her.

I don't think they knew I was behind them, looking out the open barn window at Strawberry Hill myself. In fact, they didn't seem to know there was anybody in the world except themselves. All of a sudden, I noticed Dad's left arm go around Mom's kind of roundish shoulders, and I heard him say, "But I like grayish-brown color just as well"—which is the color of Mom's hair.

Then she leaned her head on his big wide shoulder and said something to him that I couldn't hear and maybe wasn't supposed to anyway. But I guess it must have been about her hair getting gray and her not wanting it to, for Dad answered her, saying, "Everybody's life has to have a winter. That's the way God made us."

For about a whole minute neither one of them said a word, and I was quiet as a mouse. In fact, I was even quieter, because right that minute I heard a rustling above my head. Looking up, I saw on the top shelf of Dad's cupboard a pointed-nosed, beady-eyed mouse, which, I knew, if Mom saw, she'd scream the way women and girls are supposed to when they see a mouse.

I kept on being quieter than a mouse, and I was glad I did, because I heard Mom say something kind of important. It was, "I hope we can bring up our children to love the One who made those beautiful hills."

Then I saw my dad's arm tighten around her shoulders. For some reason, I felt terribly good inside, and I decided I ought to try to help Mom and Dad do what they were trying to do—and were having a hard time doing.

It was time to throw down hay for the horses, so I left the yellow-brown-furred mouse to himself and went over to the wooden ladder that leads up to our hayloft. When I got to the top, I started whistling and throwing down forkfuls of sweet-smelling alfalfa, and—do you know what?—I noticed I was whistling the same hymn I had been whistling a whole lot that summer and fall. The words of the first line were:

A mighty fortress is our God.

Suddenly it seemed He was what the song said He was, and even though He was awfully wonderful, He still had time to look after me and all of our gang. In fact, I *knew* He was interested in us when we had a very dangerous experience one cold winter day that same year.

There were maybe three inches of snow on the ground that day, nice fresh snow, very white and very clean and just right for making tracks, although the weather seemed to be getting colder fast, and the snow didn't pack well into snowballs.

The gang had been planning to spend a night up in the hills in the haunted house, if our parents would let us. We had tried hard to show them that it would be all right for us to do it. We had carried a lot of firewood into the house and stacked it in the big living room. We had even laid the fire so it would be ready to start in a hurry. Also, we had cleaned the room we had planned to sleep in. If we all took sleeping bags and blankets and had a good fire in the fireplace, it would be more fun than you could shake a stick at to stay there all night.

But our parents said we couldn't—not in the wintertime.

"Absolutely not!" Dad and all the other pops had said. All of our moms had said the same thing, only my mom said it first. Dad had seemed a little sad when he had to agree with her, but he did almost right away, and that made *me* feel sad.

So it was "absolutely not" for all of us. Middle-sized Jim had never been to the haunted house, so we decided to take him along one day to show him the upstairs and especially the attic, where we had seen the ring-tailed ghost you know about if you've read the book *The Haunted House*.

But there was too much snow on the ground for us to take Middle-sized Jim along that day, because it'd be too hard for him to walk, even if he used his crutches. Besides, it was pretty far, and he would get too tired, and none of us wanted to walk as slowly as we knew we would have to if he went with us. So we went without him.

We got into the house as we always do, through the basement and up through a trap-door into the kitchen. Then we went upstairs, where we had a lot of cold fun retelling to ourselves the exciting experiences we'd had there one dark night, scaring a ring-tailed ghost that had been making its home in the attic.

We even went into the attic and looked around a little. The first thing I noticed was that the big hole that had been in the chimney the first time we'd visited the house had been repaired.

"It's a good thing they plugged up the hole," Dragonfly said, "or if anybody started a fire in the fireplace downstairs, all the smoke'd come out here."

Along about four in the afternoon, it began to start to get dark, as it does in the wintertime, especially on a cloudy day, so we decided to get going for our different homes, which were quite a ways away.

"Let's take the shortcut home," Big Jim said, "so we can get home in time to help our folks do the chores."

The shortcut, as you know, is through Old Man Paddler's cabin and his basement and then along a long tunnel-like cave that comes out at the other end by the old sycamore tree. From the tree, we would follow Sugar Creek to most of our different homes.

It didn't take us nearly as long to get back as it had to go, because we had played nearly all the way up, the way most boys do.

It hadn't been nearly as hard walking as we thought it might be, and I was feeling kind of sad because we hadn't taken Middle-sized Jim along after all. I knew he'd feel bad about it, too, when he found out we had gone and hadn't even asked him if he wanted to go with us.

Anyway, when we got to the spring, where we had all met before we started, all of sudden Circus, who had been carrying Big Jim's rifle, said, "Hey, gang, come here! Look! There's some strange kind of animal been following our tracks up to the haunted house."

His scary-sounding voice started the red hair under my cap to moving as though it was starting to stand straight up.

We all galloped through the three-inch-deep snow to where Circus was. But, shucks, I thought, it wasn't anything. Just some kind of a human being's tracks that had come from the direction of Circus's and Big Jim's and Middle-sized Jim's houses.

"April fool," Circus said, when we had all looked disgustedly down at only a boy's tracks. "It's only a poor crippled Lion."

Well, it wasn't April first, and it didn't seem very funny. Even though I could tell by the tangled-up way the shoe tracks were made that they were Middle-sized Jim's tracks, I didn't like anybody to call him "a poor crippled Lion." I was sure Middle-sized Jim himself wouldn't like that at all. He didn't want anybody to pity him, as most handicapped and blind people don't, Dad says.

"Look everybody!" Poetry said with his squawky voice. "He's been following our tracks all right! I'll bet he found out we were going on an adventure and decided to follow us! We'd better take out after him and see if we can catch up with him and stop him."

And as soon as Big Jim had thought the idea over, we all, as quick as anything, were ready to start off.

"How long ago was he here?" Dragonfly wanted to know.

Circus, whose pop is a hunter and who trails more coon and rabbit tracks than any of the rest of us, stooped down and studied the shoe prints and said, "Maybe not more than an hour ago. See, the wind has already filled some of the Lion's tracks with snow."

And it had. Our own tracks—the ones we had made ourselves when we had started out about two o'clock—had quite a little snow blown into them. Middle-sized Jim's tracks—we were sure they were his because every now and then we saw where he had used his crutches— were a lot fresher than ours.

"Let's run," Big Jim said, "or it'll be too dark to follow his tracks. Or else maybe when he gets to some of those places where the wind has a clean sweep, he'll lose our trail and get lost, and then if we can't find him, he'll have to stay out all night in the hills and maybe freeze to death!"

That sounded like serious business. I was thinking about the "absolute concentration" that Middle-sized Jim had to have all the time when he walked or ran. If he got too cold or worried or something, he might not be able to concentrate and would have to use his crutches. He might fall down a lot of times and hurt himself. He might not even be able to get up. So if we didn't find him, he *really* would be lost and have to stay out all night in the woods in the very cold weather.

So away we all went, not stopping to think that our own folks might be worrying about us, wondering where we were and why we didn't come home.

Pretty soon we came to the old sycamore tree, where, earlier in the afternoon, we had decided not to go through the cave on our way to the haunted house but, instead, had gone on around the long way. There, in the quick gathering twilight, we stopped and looked at each other's worried faces.

Big Jim said, "He's gone on, following our tracks. I was hoping he had gone into the cave and that maybe we could follow him through and find him up in Old Man Paddler's cabin."

Little Jim, standing beside me, holding onto his ash stick, looked really concerned. I noticed that his teeth were chattering with the cold, and I wished that he, being such a little guy, were home beside a nice warm fire.

"We'd better start really running if we want to catch up with him before he gets clear up to the haunted house." Big Jim studied Middle-sized Jim's tracks. "At least he hasn't started falling down yet."

"Let's holler and see if we can make him hear," Circus said. He was able to make a terribly loud, high-pitched call that sounded both like a loon and a ghost. Right away, he let out a bloodcurdling long, weird scream. *"Ohoooo! Ohoooo!"*

We listened, but there was no answer—not even an echo—but we did hear *something*.

"What is that?" Dragonfly asked. "Sounds like a swarm of bees or an airplane or something."

And honest-to-goodness for sure, something did sound like a swarm of bees. We all listened as hard as we could. And then I began to get worried, because what we'd heard wasn't an airplane or a swarm of bees but *wind* blowing through the bare branches of the oaks and maples and elms and other trees of the Sugar Creek hills.

"We've really got to get going now," Big Jim said. "That's wind! There's a terrible storm coming up, and when it hits it'll pick up all this loose dry snow and whip it up into a blizzard! It'll cover up every track we ever made, and he'll really get lost for sure! And we can't follow *his* tracks either!"

Only one thing was right to do, and we started to do it, which was hurry like a house afire on that trail, following our old tracks and Middle-sized Jim's new ones.

"It'll be dark in only a few minutes after that wind hits!" Big Jim said.

I looked toward the highest hill, which was about a quarter of a mile away, and couldn't even see it because it had got dark that fast. All I could see was a whitish-dark cloud—which is the way a snowstorm looks at twilight before it reaches you.

We plunged headfirst on, following the path our own feet had made in the snow, watching all the time to see if Middle-sized Jim's tracks were still following them.

And then a thick formation of clouds rolled across the sky, and in almost no time it was whirling, blinding dark, and we were in the middle of a terrible blizzard. At the same time, the wind struck. It seemed the wind was acting like a giant-sized snow shovel, scooping up whole hills of snow and socking us with it. I felt it beating against my face and neck and into my collar, and I knew we were in for some very dangerous excitement.

"H-hadn't we b-better g-go back h-home?" Dragonfly asked in the whining voice he sometimes uses when he is worried. "Mother told me not to catch cold." Then he sneezed the way he does when he gets ragweed or goldenrod pollen in his nose or when he gets too close to a horse and smells its dandruffy hair.

Well, it's a queer feeling being out in the woods among the hills when a howling, blinding snowstorm is all around you, when you can't see more than a few yards in any direction, and when you know you are a long way from home and from any kind of shelter—also when it's not only cold but is getting colder every minute.

"We've got to find Middle-sized Jim and save him!" Big Jim gasped.

Dragonfly yelled back above the storm, holding his hand up to his mouth to keep from inhaling the cold air direct into his allergic bronchial tubes, "We've got to save ourselves!"

For once Dragonfly was right. We all seemed to know it at the same time. And in that blinding, madly whirling blizzard, every direction seemed like every other direction.

"Hey, you guys!" I heard Big Jim yell. "Come here! Quick!"

We struggled through the snow and crowded around him in a little gasping, panting huddle, wondering what he was going to tell us.

Also, I was looking around in the snow to see if maybe he had found Middle-sized Jim.

Then in a voice that was pretty excited for Big Jim's voice, he said, "We're lost! All our tracks are already covered up with snow!"

It was a sickening feeling, hearing that and knowing we really *were* lost.

But Big Jim certainly wasn't any sissy. He raised his voice so that he could be sure all of us heard him and said, "Two things, gang. First, we are to stick together, so if we can't find the stone house where we'll be sheltered from this terrible storm, we can huddle close together and help keep each other warm. And second, we've got to find our directions so we'll know which way to go."

It made sense. I knew we wouldn't have any trouble staying together, but who could tell what direction it was without any daylight or any sun and without a compass? Every boy who spends a lot of time in the woods or anyplace where he might get lost ought to carry a compass.

"Any of you have a compass? Poetry, you got yours?"

Poetry sometimes carried one with him. Also, on our hikes he always carried a waterproof matchbox.

Poetry tried all his pockets and didn't have his compass. "I must have left it in my other pants," he said, which is what a boy does with a lot of different things when he changes clothes.

I shoved my hands into my pockets, too, and pulled out a buckeye and a papaw seed, then shoved my hands back in again and left them there to keep them warm.

Well, that was that. We didn't have any compass, and there was no way of knowing what direction to go to find the old stone house. It was so blinding dark on account of the swirling, driving snow that we couldn't see more than a half-dozen white yards in front of us.

Little Jim was close beside me. I looked at his face, which so much of the time is as innocent as a lamb's face, but this time it wasn't. His small jaw was set as though he was getting ready to dive through a tangle of football players, and then all of a surprising sudden, he said, "If we can find a tree, we can tell which way *north* is."

"If we can find what?" Circus said.

"If we can find a tree—" Little Jim was interrupted by a savage gust of wind that whipped in and cut off his breath.

As you maybe know, Little Jim was always studying nature, looking for and finding wild flowers and weeds and different kinds of trees and writing their names in his notebook. So I thought maybe he might have a bright idea. When he got his breath again, he said, "If we can find a tree, we can tell which way *north* is, because the thickest moss and lichen grow on the bark on the north side."

Well, as long as I have lived at Sugar Creek, where there are hundreds and hundreds of trees, I'd never thought about that, but the minute Little Jim said it, I knew it was true.

Also the minute he said it, Big Jim seemed to remember it was so—he having been a Boy Scout. Right away he said, "That's right. Everybody hold onto everybody till we come to a tree," which we did.

It was a white birch with bark as white as snow, but it had big patches of green lichen on one side all up and down its trunk. We studied it up close and also several other trees nearby, just to be sure that all of them had patches of lichen on the same side. And that's how we found out which way *north* was.

But that didn't help us much. We still didn't know what direction we were from the stone house. If we'd been as well acquainted with this part of Sugar Creek territory as we were with that section of it that was closer to our homes, it'd have been easy.

Circus got a bright idea then. He said, "What direction were we going when the storm hit while we were still following our tracks?"

"Southwest," Big Jim said. "That old house is southwest of the sycamore tree, and we were going toward it."

Little Jim's cheerful voice called out right then. I heard him say, "If we keep on watching the north sides of the trees, we can tell which way to keep on going!"

And so we plunged on again, going southwest, following Big Jim and Circus, who were breaking trail for us. The walking got harder, and I kept stumbling over snow-covered logs and underbrush and falling down, even worse maybe than Middle-sized Jim would have done.

I don't know what the rest of the gang was thinking about while we were struggling and gasping and plunging into and out of and through those drifts, but because I liked Middle-sized Jim very much, I kept wondering if he had managed to get to the house before the storm struck. And had he found out we weren't there and already started back on the other trail? Was he maybe lying flat in the snow some-where, unable to get up? What if we couldn't find him at all, and he would have to stay out all night? Why, he would freeze to death! It was a terribly sad thought.

Also, I was thinking something else, but I probably wouldn't have written it down for you if Little Jim hadn't been thinking the same and said it to me out loud. This is what it was: "I wonder if Middle-sized Jim is a Christian."

I didn't know for sure.

Dragonfly heard Little Jim say that, and he gasped out a wheezy answer, "A Christian would freeze to death the same as anybody else, if he had to stay all night in this kind of weather."

I knew Dragonfly was right. Cold weather would be cold for a Christian the same as for anybody else.

It made it seem very important, though, that we find Middle-sized Jim, so without know-ing I was going to do it, I yelled at the top of my lungs, calling Middle-sized Jim's name. But I could hardly hear myself. My voice sounded as dead as if I had thrown it into a lot of whirling goose feathers, on account of the roaring wind. And of course there wasn't any answer from Middle-sized Jim.

I'll have to admit I was pretty scared, for myself as well as for Middle-sized Jim. Every single member of the Sugar Creek Gang was already a Christian, because we'd already shoved open the doors of our different hearts and had let the Savior come in, and He had washed all of us from all our sins. I knew that if we had to freeze to death, we would all go straight to heaven, but I certainly didn't want to go there that afternoon.

While I stumbled and plunged along behind Big Jim and some of the rest of the gang, I thought about my grayish-brown-haired mom. And then I even imagined that if none of our gang came home, Dad would get up a searching party as soon as the storm was over enough so he could, and he and a lot of men would come out looking for us. And maybe they'd find us out here in the snow, huddled together and all frozen stiff.

There'd be a funeral for all of us in the Sugar Creek church. Sylvia's pop would preach the sermon, and my dad and mom would walk slowly past the casket where their red-haired, freckle-faced boy would be lying. But only my body would be there. My spirit would be in heaven where all saved people's souls go the minute they die.

Before I got through imagining all that, I heard Circus, who was leading the way with Big Jim, let out a yell, saying, "Hey, gang! We're there! There's the old haunted house!"

8

That great big old awkward-looking stone house certainly looked good to me. I was so cold and so windblown with powdered snow all over me—and so also were all of us—that it was going to be wonderful to get inside. We would build a roaring fire in the fireplace, and all of us would get thawed out.

I almost forgot about Middle-sized Jim but only for a minute. When we got to the house, we found him sprawled by the door, panting for breath. He was as helpless as a small wood turtle is when you turn him over on his back in a slippery place and he gets all his four legs working at the same time trying to turn back on his stomach and can't.

We went into quick action. In less time than it would take me to tell you about it, we all rushed to Middle-sized Jim's rescue and got him, along with the rest of our very cold selves, into the basement entrance, up through the trapdoor into the kitchen, and on into the large living room where the fireplace was and where, in a few minutes, we would have a fire going.

It was almost dark inside, but it would be easy to start a fire. When we had been planning and hoping we could stay all night, we had taken some straight slivers of split sticks and some shredded bark and made a little wigwam of them in the fireplace. Also we had stood up some larger pieces of wood all around them, so that all we would have to do would be to touch a match to it. As soon as it was going good, we'd lay larger pieces of wood on it and then some fireplace logs, which we had carried in. Pretty soon, we'd be as warm as toast.

I couldn't help but think how maybe we'd get to stay here all night after all.

Gasping and panting and still terribly cold, we felt our way around in the almost-dark house.

Middle-sized Jim said, "I've got a flashlight in my pocket, so you can see to start the fire."

"How come you got a flashlight?" Poetry's squawky voice asked.

And Middle-sized Jim replied, "I keep it all the time so if I fall down somewhere outdoors at night, I can flash it on and off, and my father can tell where I am."

Well, as cold as it was, and as cold as we still were, it looked like we were going to have a happy adventure. Of course, we would have to keep our fire burning all night and maybe all day tomorrow too, until the storm stopped long enough for us to go home or until our folks or somebody else came to rescue us.

"Now, for a good warm fire," Big Jim said, walking over to a corner and leaning his empty .22 rifle there. Big Jim never carried his gun loaded unless we were actually hunting. Then he turned to Poetry and said cheerfully, "OK, fireman, let's have the matches."

Middle-sized Jim was sitting on the floor near the rifle, and Big Jim was holding the pocket flashlight on Poetry, who quick shoved one hand into his pocket for his waterproof matchbox.

And then I saw the most puzzled expression come over Poetry's face. Before any of us had time to think, he came to life, and both of his hands were acting excited, diving in and out of first one pocket and then another. Even before he said a word, I knew he didn't have a single match.

And right that minute, it seemed I had never been so cold in my life. The wind outside was whistling and moaning and howling. Snow was driving in through a crack in the window behind me. Every single one of us searched his pockets, and there wasn't a match among us— not even one!

Not a match among us! Zero weather! A howling blizzard and absolutely no way to start a fire!

Well, what can you do when there isn't a thing you can do? In some of the fastest remembering I had ever done, I remembered a time, one cold winter day, when we had all gone up to see Old Man Paddler in his cabin. When we got there, we found him in his cellar—he had fallen down the steps. The fire was out in the house, and there wasn't even one match to start a fire then either.

We had saved the old man and ourselves

from freezing by taking one of the lenses of his reading glasses, which were as thick as magnifying glasses, and holding it in the sunlight just above some dry, decayed wood. Big Jim had kept on holding it there, blowing on it at the same time until there was a reddish glow in the punk, which is the name for that kind of dried, decayed wood. The little glow grew bigger and brighter as Big Jim kept on blowing on it, moving the spot of light around a little so the fire would spread. Then he took a piece of rolled-up tissue paper, touched it to the live coal, blowing on it at the same time, and—*presto-chango!* Just like that, all of a sudden there was a flame! Minutes later, we had a roaring fire in the old man's fireplace.

But there wasn't any sunlight in an old stone house in the middle of a Sugar Creek blizzard.

"We could start a fire by friction like Indians do, if we had a bow and arrow," Dragonfly said, his teeth chattering from the cold.

Big Jim turned the idea over in his mind. But we didn't have any bow, and even if we had, the thong would have to be made out of leather, and we didn't have any, although maybe we could have cut a long strip of leather from one of our belts. We would also need a soapstone, which we didn't have. Even if any of us had known for sure *how* to start a fire by friction, we didn't have the materials with which to do it anyway.

It was still not quite dark in the house,

because of the white snow outside, so we could see each other's face a little, even when we didn't have the flashlight turned on.

"Are there any blankets anywhere?" Middle-sized Jim asked, his voice trembling. I noticed he was shivering pitifully. He was probably colder than any of the rest of us because we had been running and fighting against the storm right up until the last minute, while he had been lying helpless outside the door, not able to get up.

I guess I never felt so sorry for a person in my life as I did for that good-hearted boy. I knew there weren't any blankets, and I hated to have to tell him, but I did and sat down beside him to help him get warm.

Little red-haired Tom Till spoke up and said, "Maybe some of our folks will come for us."

"Not tonight they won't," Poetry said. "Nobody could walk in this wind."

We didn't want to use up all the battery in Middle-sized Jim's flashlight, so we turned it off and stared at each other in the light-dark. We huddled close together and listened to the wind howl and moan and the snow beat against the windows. I felt myself shivering and shivering.

"We'd better keep moving," Big Jim said, "or we'll freeze."

It was a good idea, except that, of course, Middle-sized Jim couldn't walk very well, and he couldn't swing his arms around and beat them against his sides as the rest of us could.

All the while, time was passing. The wind sounded like a lot of angry wild animals, and the snow, pounding against the windows, sounded as if somebody was out there throwing sand against them. I began to feel desperate. We couldn't go home, and we didn't have a match or a thing to start a fire with.

"Looks like we're going to get to do what we wanted to do," Big Jim said, but he didn't say it very cheerfully.

It certainly wasn't a happy prospect. If there is anything in the world that makes you feel discouraged, it is to be too cold and not have any way to get warm.

"There ought to be just one match around here *somewhere*," Big Jim said.

All of us went through all our pockets again. I went through all thirteen of mine—four in my trousers, four in my overalls that were over my trousers, four in my mackinaw, and one in my shirt. In no time, all eight of us had searched all of our nearly one hundred pockets, and there wasn't a match among us.

If we had emptied out all the stuff we did have, it'd have made a big pile. We had things such as coins, buckeyes, papaw seeds, knives, nails, nuts and bolts, pieces of string, pencils, pens, and other stuff that boys always carry—enough maybe to start a secondhand store in Sugar Creek.

I noticed that Big Jim had a small box of .22 caliber cartridges for his rifle. Little Jim and three or four of the rest of us had our small, thin, leather New Testaments.

Seeing mine, I was reminded that there was a God and that if nobody among us could do anything about getting a fire started, *He* could show us what to do. I knew that if Sylvia's pop had been there, he would probably ask us to bow our heads and shut our eyes, and he'd say, as he sometimes does at church, "Let us all pray." I also thought that since God had made the world and all the boys in it, He could answer prayer and help us get a fire started so we could get warm. But Sylvia's pop wasn't there.

Most of us put our stuff back in our pockets, except Little Jim, who, I noticed, kept his New Testament out, holding it half hidden in one of his hands.

I got a fine surprise, though, when Big Jim said in a voice that sounded almost as if he was angry, "Do we all claim to be Christians, or don't we?"

Not a one of us answered him, but I felt myself swallowing something in my throat. I glanced down at Little Jim's New Testament and noticed that he was holding it terribly tight.

Then Big Jim said, "If any of our dads was here, we'd ask him if he had a match or if he could help us start a fire, wouldn't we?"

Still not a one of us answered a word.

Big Jim spoke again in a firm voice. "All right, then, our dads aren't here, but we all know who is. Everybody bow his head, shut his eyes, and keep still. Let each one pray his own silent prayer."

Quick as anything, all our heads went down. I didn't know I had my cap off, even as cold as it was, until I felt it in my hands. Then I remembered that is the polite thing to do when you pray.

I guess I didn't say much of a prayer except to ask God to do anything He could about the Sugar Creek Gang and especially for Middle-sized Jim, who was sort of leaning against me and shaking with the cold.

I didn't suppose any of us would pray out loud, although at the Sugar Creek church, when we have what is called Bible Treasure Club, different ones of us sometimes did, even though we were as bashful as anything about doing it.

But suddenly I heard Big Jim's voice, and he was making as nice a prayer as anybody in the church could have made. Part of it was: "We're just a bunch of worried boys who have to have help, and we know You can do anything. If there is any way we can help ourselves, please show us what it is, and we'll try to do it. Bless our folks and help them not to worry, but it does look like we'll have to have a fire or we'll freeze."

The word "freeze" seemed to make me shiver a little harder than I had been.

Big Jim hadn't any sooner finished his prayer than Dragonfly spoke up with what sounded like the absolutely dumbest thing he had ever said in his life. It was, "Whyn't we do like the Indians do and make a smoke signal for our folks to see, and then—"

That was as far as he got. Circus interrupted, saying, "You're crazy! How can you get smoke without a fire? That's what we have to have—a fire!"

"I was trying to be funny," Dragonfly said.

And Circus said, "You didn't try hard enough. But if you'd try being crazy once, you wouldn't have to try so hard."

Anyway, when Dragonfly mentioned smoke, Little Jim spoke up and said, "You could get a *little* smoke if you would shoot Big Jim's rifle." Then, as though he knew his idea wasn't any good, he added, "But nobody would see it."

But the very minute Little Jim said what he said, Big Jim jumped as if he had been shot at and hit. He looked quick at Middle-sized Jim and exclaimed, "That book on outdoor life you let me read—wasn't there something in it about starting a fire? You know—like lost hunters do sometimes when they haven't any matches?"

"That's too dangerous for a boy," Middle-sized Jim said. His voice was trembling, and he was actually shaking with the cold.

Big Jim's face was set grimly, and it seemed he was feeling responsible for all of us—he being the leader. "It wouldn't be as dangerous as freezing to death," he said.

What wouldn't? I thought but didn't say anything.

And then I heard Big Jim mumbling to himself, as he beat his mittened hands together to keep the circulation going. A moment later, he said, "I've got to do it—danger or no danger!" Then he raised his voice and said to all of us, "There's only one way for us to start a fire, and it's very dangerous!"

Just as he finished saying that, there was a banging upstairs or on the roof or somewhere, like a tree branch breaking off in the wind and falling on the house. That noise seemed to help Big Jim to make up his mind, because right away he started doing things.

"Here goes," he said almost savagely. He quick shoved a hand into one of his pockets and pulled out his box of .22 caliber cartridges, and a second later he had one of them in his cold, shivering hand.

"Be *careful!*" Dragonfly exclaimed excitedly. "It might go off!"

"I know it," Big Jim answered, "but I don't think it will if I am careful. You guys step back —all but Circus. Circus, you hold the flashlight for me."

All of us got back a few feet.

With both worried eyes, I watched Big Jim. I could see the muscles of his jaw working, and his face was tense. His fuzzy upper lip seemed to be trembling, and maybe his teeth were chattering too. And I knew it wasn't because of the cold weather but was because what he was going to do was very dangerous.

Circus's hand that was holding the small

flashlight was trembling too. I noticed that part of the flashlight's beam went on past the small copper cartridge Big Jim was holding and lit up the fireplace, which had in it shredded bark and fine wood shavings as well as larger pieces of wood.

Big Jim's hands were almost fiery red with cold, and they seemed so numb that he was having a hard time doing what he wanted to do with the cartridge. "Here," he said. "Hold it a minute, while I get my hands warm."

He laid the cartridge in Circus's palm and straightened up. Then he stepped toward the center of the room, shoved his hands back into his mittens, and began swinging his arms round and round his body and beating his hands together to get the blood circulating again.

Then he quick took off his mittens and, taking the small copper cartridge in his fingers, started working and worrying at the lead bullet in it, twisting carefully and pulling. All of a sudden the bullet came out, and he had the shell with the powder in it in one hand and the bullet in the other.

"Here, Bill," he said, handing it to me. "Hold this bullet."

I took the lead bullet in my hand, knowing that by itself it wasn't dangerous to hold, no more than if I'd found a piece of lead along Sugar Creek.

The next thing Big Jim did was to very carefully pour out most of the black powder from the shell—being extra careful not to spill any—

onto the windowsill on the opposite side of the room from the fireplace. In fact, he poured it into a little patch of powdered snow. "It'll get wet in the snow," he said, "and won't be dangerous. After we get the fire started in the fireplace, we'll throw it out into the storm."

What he was doing still didn't make sense. I couldn't see how in the world he could get a fire started that way. But he acted as if he knew what he was doing. The rest of us, except Circus, stayed where we were and watched—and maybe helped a little by praying, although I didn't feel I was a good enough boy for God to answer, even if I *was* a Christian.

I kept thinking about the powder being easily ignited and very dangerous, and I was glad Big Jim was being careful. If that powder exploded in his hands it might give him a terribly bad powder burn. It might even put out his eyes, as firecrackers do when they explode in a boy's hands too close to his eyes. Of course, we had all fired firecrackers on the Fourth of July, but that was different. They had fuses on them, and none of us were ever close to them when they exploded.

"Now," Big Jim said, "who wants to sacrifice a small strip of his cotton shirttail? It's got to be cotton."

"I don't," Dragonfly said. "Mother would give me a licking if anybody cut a hole in my shirt."

"Here's mine," Little Jim said, and he already had his coat unbuttoned and his shirttail out in front.

Big Jim ordered Poetry, "You snip off a very small strip and make it into a wad the size of a small garden pea."

It still didn't make sense. How could anybody start a fire with a practically empty shell and a piece of a boy's shirttail?

Quicker than anything, Poetry had his Scout knife out and a small piece of Little Jim's green-and-white-striped shirttail cut off and wadded into a tiny ball.

Very carefully then, Big Jim plugged that pea-sized piece of cotton shirttail into the end of the cartridge where the bullet had been. Then I saw his jaw set firmly as he straightened up and said, "Now we're ready. Hand me the rifle."

His rifle, as you know, was leaning against the wall in the corner. It wasn't loaded, as I've already told you, because Big Jim knew how to be careful with a gun, that being one of the reasons his folks let him own one.

Quickly he had the gun loaded with the shirttail bullet.

"You going to *shoot* a fire into the fireplace?" Dragonfly asked.

When I heard that, the whole idea began to make sense to me.

"No," Big Jim answered Dragonfly. "The smoke and the force of the wind might blow our shredded bark away. I've got a better idea."

The next few minutes were the most interesting ones I'd had in a long time, although I was shivering with the cold and worrying as much as I could, and maybe I was praying a little bit too.

"Attention, everybody," Big Jim ordered. "I'm going to shoot this cotton bullet straight toward the ceiling. It can't start a fire up there because the ceiling is plaster. But the cotton bullet *will* come down in the room here somewhere, and it will be smoldering, like a firecracker does after it has gone off. Don't anybody touch it. I'll take care of it."

I could feel my heart pounding fast as he held the gun with the muzzle toward the dark ceiling.

"Watch it, now!" Big Jim said grimly.

Dragonfly, beside me, grabbed his nose, because the smell of smoking gunpowder always made him sneeze.

Then Big Jim pulled the trigger, and I saw a spit of flame shoot up into the air out of the rifle's muzzle, and at the same time Little Jim's piece of shirttail flew up to the ceiling. A second later it plopped down, smoldering right close to Poetry.

Big Jim pounced upon it, whisked it up in his leather-palmed mitten, dashed to the fireplace with it, and laid it right in the center of the dry tinder. In terribly fast time, he was down on his knees, aiming the flashlight on the little pile of tinder with the smoking piece of Little Jim's shirttail in the center of it, and was blowing on it.

And then, what to my wondering eyes should appear but a little yellow flame shooting up from the tinder! Then there were more flames, and bigger ones, and I began to hear the very cheerful crackling noise a live fire always makes, and I knew our lives were saved.

We knew we would have to stay in the house all night—or most of it anyway—so as soon as we got warmer, we began to have fun talking it all over and even laughing about it. Middle-sized Jim had certainly turned out to be a very interesting boy to have with us. In fact, if he hadn't followed our trail, we wouldn't have followed his, and we wouldn't have got to stay all night in the haunted house, as we had wanted to do in the first place.

After we got completely thawed out, Big Jim said to us, as he sat on the floor with the firelight flickering on his fuzzy upper lip, "I guess we owe a vote of thanks to Somebody, don't we?"

His saying "Somebody" in the serious way he said it made me know who he meant, and it also made me feel good inside. Right away my thoughts jumped clear over the tops of the blizzard-swept hills and way back to the Sugar Creek church where we all went every Sunday.

My thoughts were interrupted when Poetry said, "What's that song you're whistling, Bill?"

It was just like it had been that other day when I had been whistling without knowing it. I thought a second, and part of the tune was still in my mind. It was the same one I'd whistled a lot of times that summer and fall and winter. I knew Poetry knew the name of the song, so I wasn't going to tell him.

I wouldn't have needed to anyway, because all of a sudden, Middle-sized Jim answered for me, saying, "That's Martin Luther's famous hymn 'A Mighty Fortress Is Our God.' He wrote it over four hundred years ago, after he had been reading the forty-sixth psalm in the Bible. The first line of it is on the tombstone in Germany where he is buried—I read it in a book my folks gave me when I became a Christian."

Hearing him say that made me look quick at Little Jim just as he looked quick at me. Little Jim took a deep breath and sighed, and I thought his face looked as if he was very glad inside.

In fact, I felt fine myself on account of the wonderful way God had made everything turn out. As I sat with the cold air pushing against my back and with the fire pushing its very friendly heat against my face, there was a warm feeling in my heart toward Him, not only because He had saved our lives but because He really liked me. And it didn't make any difference about Middle-sized Jim's being handicapped—He liked him just as much as if he were a boy with a perfect body.

Dragonfly spoke up just then and said—sneezing right before he said it—"My folks might take me down South after Christmas and let me go to school down there where I won't get so many colds and sneeze so much and have to miss so much school."

I looked at his kind of pinched face and wished he didn't have to stay up North in the cold Sugar Creek winter. In fact, I'd sort of like to go to a warm climate myself, I thought. And —just like that!—I began to hope that if Dragonfly's parents decided to take him down to Texas or Arizona or Florida or somewhere for a month or two during the coldest part of the winter, maybe some of our parents would let us go too, even if we couldn't stay.

Boy oh boy, that would be wonderful! Why, down South they not only had warm weather in the winter, but there were a million things for a boy to see and do! If you went far enough, you could go fishing in the Gulf of Mexico and catch a fish as big as a boy!

If Dragonfly *does* go and any of the rest of us get to go to visit him, I'll tell you about it. Imagine catching a fish as big as a boy!